W9-BEC-802

The Really Rotten Princess

by Lady Cecily Snodgrass
illustrated by Mike Lester

Ready-to-Read

Simon Spotlight
New York London Toronto Sydney New Delhi

SIMON SPOTLIGHT
An imprint of Simon & Schuster Children's Publishing Division
1230 Avenue of the Americas, New York, New York 10020

Copyright © 2012 by Simon & Schuster, Inc.
All rights reserved, including the right of reproduction in whole or in part in any form.
SIMON SPOTLIGHT, READY-TO-READ, and colophon are registered trademarks of
Simon & Schuster, Inc.

For information about special discounts for bulk purchases, please contact Simon & Schuster
Special Sales at 1-866-506-1949 or business@simonandschuster.com.
Manufactured in the United States of America 0112 LAK
First Edition
10 9 8 7 6 5 4 3 2 1
Library of Congress Cataloging-in-Publication Data
Snodgrass, Cecily.
Really rotten princess / by Lady Cecily Snodgrass ; illustrated by Mike
Lester. — 1st ed.
p. cm. — (Ready-to-read)
Summary: Princess Regina, whose behavior is abominable, is sent to a
boarding school to learn how to act like a proper princess.
ISBN 978-1-4424-3325-0 (pbk. : alk. paper) — ISBN 978-1-4424-3326-7
(hardcover : alk. paper)
[1. Princesses—Fiction. 2. Behavior—Fiction. 3. Schools—Fiction.] I.
Lester, Mike, ill. II. Title.
PZ7.S68032Re 2011
[E]—dc23
2011028306
ISBN 978-1-4424-3327-4 (eBook)

Once upon a time . . .
about three weeks ago . . .
there lived a princess
named Regina.

But unlike most princesses,
Regina was not very nice.

In fact, she was downright rotten.

Instead of tapping someone gently with her scepter, she would bonk them on the head as hard as she could.

At tea parties she would give her guests salt for their tea in place of sugar.

And she thought it was *really* funny to mislabel the magic powders of the court wizard, Maldemar.

But like all parents of really rotten kids, the king and queen thought she was perfect.

Then one day Regina overheard
Maldemar telling her parents
that maybe it was time
to send her to a special
school for princesses.

Like all really rotten kids,
it never occurred to Regina
that the people she was nasty
to might try to get back at her.

In the end they decided
it was a good idea.

Regina was not happy as she packed.

She was not happy as her subjects wished her farewell.

DON'T COME BACK!

YOU'RE NASTY!

GOOD RIDDANCE!

And Regina was definitely not happy when she arrived at Miss Priscilla Prunerot's school for princesses.

Miss Priscilla Prunerot's PAINSTAKINGLY PERFECT PREPARATORY SCHOOL FOR Princesses

For the first time she realized
that she was not the only princess
in the world.

There were all kinds of princesses at the school.

There was a princess with really, really long hair.

There was a princess who slept all the time.

There was a fairy princess who sprinkled pixie dust everywhere.

And there was another princess who swept it all up.

z z z z

There was a princess who had her own genie!

And there was even a princess who had a pet dragon.

To make matters worse,
Regina found she didn't
even have her own room!

Princess Sweet Pea was so sensitive, she needed nine mattresses to protect her from feeling one little pea.

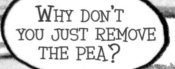

Princess Seafoam showed both girls
her prized collection of magical
spiny seashells.
But she wouldn't tell
what their magic was.

The first day of school was filled with lessons.

They learned how to polish tiaras.

They were taught the proper way to address peasants.

They practiced spinning gold from straw.

And they learned the correct way to wave to their subjects.

That night in bed Regina suddenly realized she hadn't done anything rotten the entire day.

So she decided to do something about it.

The next morning Regina removed
the pea from Princess Sweet Pea's
bed. She replaced it with Princess
Seafoam's spiny seashells.
But that wasn't all she did. . . .

A class learning to sing with woodland creatures found that their bluebirds had been replaced with bats.

And when they practiced
how to run from princes
while wearing glass slippers,
they found someone had spread
grease on the floor.

And worst of all, someone had put superglue on the lips of every frog in their afternoon frog-kissing class.

Miss Prunerot announced that whoever had done these dire deeds would be punished when caught.

Princess Seafoam said her magic
seashells could tell them who did it.
But the shells were missing.

AAAIIIIEEEE!!!

Later that night Princess Sweet
Pea found the shells.

The shells really were magic. They could answer any question Princess Seafoam asked them.

And they did!

As punishment, Regina had to
clean the Royal Unicorn Stables.
But she didn't even mind. The
shells had given her a name that
she secretly liked—the Really
Rotten Princess.